for
butter rabbit

and 9

Amphitheater

煦 (Susie Zhu)

This is an experiment conducted on the generative model of the Fibonacci sequence.

On the 1st day, 1 (**rabbit/writing/girl**) is inserted into this compact enclosed space of a (**poem/stage/darkroom**). On the 2nd, an additional mirror is installed (since there must be 2 to begin with.)

You are invited to be among its audience as it develops and expands and overflows the frame (it is impossible to put a period to an autonomous sentence mechanism of water...but unlike the one trapped in multiple, you can always exit. Simply by closing the (**curtain/book/bracket**).

On the 11th day you (**leave/will leave/will have left**).

End of Prologue

I[1]

There, we recognize a *pond*, for lack of a better word.

---

[1]

"no one can see their reflection in running water: only in
still water that we can see"   *"best to be like water"*
(Lao Zi, *Dao De Jing*)

                     still water

looks   into water
and nothing is unobserved

in a grand void.

The lack   and omnipresence
of voice.
In water,

the stage is set.

I[2]

A young woman in yellow is at the center of the stage.

---

[2]

"une jeune femme en jaune *au coeur* de la scène."
—It could have been this that he said.

But I know little French.
And besides, with the heavy *door* separating us it is close to impossible to discern his words. So I decided to make up something for him. Like I am making up everything for myself.

2

It's about midnight. It's high noon, she thinks to herself. From the murky navy ranges of silhouettes far far behind and the moonlit branches, one could assume reasonably most public spaces should have closed already at this point—except for those intended for this very vacuity before the Sun reenters, glamorously, generously, pouring out to his people like Bacchus. A pool is usually not one of those places, of course. But for some reason, they overlooked her. So there she is, still floating, in the middle of the water, in her bright yellow ring. She stares into the cold and concrete silence in front of her, thinking to fill it with her smoldered words. She stares, long and firmly.

3

She is in the middle of the water. Yellow, circular.
[MOVE CLOSER. ZOOM IN]

She's been observing the shapes from here for a while, their movement never escapes her eyes even when they appear to be static—even when they are hardly perceptible. Like breathing in synchronicity with the trembling in the air. Or even to a molecular level of subtlety, like thermal motion. From that static face among them, she notices language emerging from this subtlety: a language so familiar, almost an echo, to her ears.

The language also gilded in a yellow nimbus.

She feels this urge of language sprouting but on her own tongue, and not long after she comes to realization: *she is me.*

But she looks so pale, so detached, so trapped in this saturation (yellow) of contemplation. Should I dive down further? Call out to her? Would she be alarmed or dispelled? Would I?

A giant fish jolts awake from its dream, panting.

5

The stage is set up as a *bedroom,* but a bedroom specifically for vertical sleep.

[AERIEAL VIEW]
(sic)

It is the ceiling which is in fact the fourth wall torn away.

The stage is designed to be a window looking onto itself from above, like the one we see upon landing into consciousness, returning from a long, exhausting foreign dream.

It is not horribly unusual a scene if you recall those matchbox dollhouses sometimes found in vintage shops and hanged tapestries on the walls. Or walls embellished with tiles, or wall papers that pretend to be tiles, or *scales that pretend to be tiles*—silvery, greasy, rendering the room a descent, touch of mystery and perversity, reminiscent of sea or the lack of it.

In this room, each tile an eye thirsty, looking out for the spray, moisture, ambiguity...

Or, occasionally, exquisite architectural plans people put on their bedroom walls (but why would anyone want to disturb their palace of repose like this? It would still make some more sense if they were found in a bureau...). A plan never ceases from speaking, rambling. Sometimes it gives her a headache. A plan utters an alternative spatiality through speaking space into the space it resides. It not only describes the space but attempts to persuade you into believing the superiority of its space over yours. But if it truly is more authentic, why must it hide behind the cloak of two-dimensionality? What is a house that pretends to be accommodated within a house after all? She thinks to herself.

A plan.

The bedroom is set up as a plan, but one that's awfully executed. Flat, even flatter than lines and dots, flatter than words, escaping every possible level of stability. Surreal. Volatile and malleable as a concept—except for the mirror installed in the middle of the room. The only one who speaks into *another* space.

She finds herself in the mirror, in a silky daffodil colored dress way too long for her that drapes all the way down to the ground, piling up between she and her other self, like the 1001 faces in water Narcissus had no clue which one he'd lost upon peering down, the golden? (*a golden fruit for the beautiful darling!*) the silver? (*fishy, fishy...*) or the rotten self?   .

Behind her a thick and inky darkness is seeping through all four corners, interrupting the performance of flatness on the stage. It distends, pushing everything out of its way, pushing her forward, toward, against the mirror, toward suffocation.

In the mirror, her eyes still closed. She sees neither the darkness nor herself approaching.

This is a mirror for us, not for her. We are offered sight, she is not.

We are not sure if she is still awake or alive.

A clock strikes twelve.

8

A square-shaped darkness

in the middle of this white space, but wavering.
It reminds you of Rothko.

You try to distinguish between the different language of the darkness. In
the wavering you feel like spotting the unraveling of their lineages, but
soon the lines get devoured back into the nameless sum.

It appears to be a piece of sea, somehow captured and inlaid awkwardly
(perhaps unwillingly) into the floor. (Who put it here?) What an odd tile.
You think. A neatly tailored fragment of nocturnal sea, dark, dense, im-
penetrable by sight, undefined.

It seems more plausible to you that it has decided to enter the room itself
one day and only then flowed all the way to the edges of the—now you
see walls around the dark square and realized that it could simply have
been badly lit a room that is sitting in the middle of this scene.

You were too engulfed by its squared immensity, the smell of salty sea
breeze you could almost smell; how a limited sight gestures to the infinite; too engulfed by the possibility of this cookie-cut sea conceiving of
you when you are trying your best to imagine it does not exist. You were
absolutely enthralled. And felt like losing it.

So enthralled that you ignored the more obvious elements: Of course there are walls around it.

You feel a great relief. Of course. How could one make a carpet out of sea? Could anything be at once fluid and rigid and docile enough to be imprisoned to this narrow page?

The room itself is quite compact as well
—approximately twice as large as the table in its center. Tightly the attic of night. Wavering. Maybe among the best places for resting.

A square-shaped slumber.
Or a bedroom.

It could only be a bedroom. But in reality it does seem to include every function of a fully furnished house [illustration: hotel suite room advertisement, toolbox laid open, X-ray for a cake.]

You imagine a girl sleeping on top of the table while another soaks into the sea beneath it. And another, stares into it, gloomy, as if looking out on yet another rainy day. Why always the water. And another, dines, in front of the sleeping girl with fork and knife in her hands. For some reason the dinning girl appears to be the most incongruous with the room among them. How bizarre.

A girl *is* dining at the table.

Someone made her breakfast and made her sit there until she is done with it. No way to know what they made for her: when you see her, only honey colored liquid remains in her plate. A small lake of thick tears? Very thick, and slow tears. With the, consistency, of, memory…Very, far…off…

And a single daffodil cowers
in a beak shaped vase at her feet, drooping.

She alone occupies the room, but it is obvious that she is not the owner. Nor does she have any autonomy. Her face so blank as if worn away by a certain rigorous repetitive act. Her tongue burnt and she could not speak in intelligible words from an over-consumption of *early suns*. Her eyes so tired of adjusting over and over to the facsimiles of light in countless mid-nights that eventually, she decided to never open them:
They made her only breakfast so she has no choice but to feel like waking up, and waking up again; feel like, dreaming, *constant dreaming*, escaping from one but only to another, to another that is the sum of whatever has already visited; feel herself turned into *stones*, pensive stones, not that of Sisyphus but of Medusa. A petrification of hope and instant annihilation. Feverish stones, sad stones.

She tried to stand up, but would always fall back, into sleep, in the same chair—the ground lulls, wavering. So does every other sea.

How long has her been in this place?

The flower has withered 144 times at her feet, very absolutely dead, but the number's still *growing*.

Her cutleries kept slipping from her drowsy fingers, dropping onto the surging waters the way rain falls into sea. *Without a sound.*

In this uncanny silence, everything in her room threads through time, but without her. An improvisation excluding her—outside her. She sits still, still. Stiller than the night drenched in the waters. Her sight fixed onto the dream she has been given, even though she sees nothing but darkness there.

It is more like the unbearably long tunnel of night before the visit of a dream, but she knows this is no more than a metaphor. Because she is in the dream. And not a single dream is empty. It must be someone that has turned off the lights.

(She is a watchman.)

(And they are here to make sure she is not escaping from her duty: They watch over her watching.)

They seem to be satisfied with what they see.

She is looking for something there, in this reflective emptiness in front of her.

Square-shaped emptiness.

All of a sudden her eyes sharpen.
She is seeing something.

At once, her face husked from the lurking drowse. This one glimpse ignites her blind dream with a flood of light, endowing her with another powerful dream. In this dream her limbs are nimble with force again; in this dream, she breaks away from the sitting dream and runs straight toward *it*, the dream she spotted. In her sight: a face, of a girl. The face she has always wanted to see.

She cuts through the frame of darkness, all the way down the dry narrow path sliced open in front of her, through all the seats, audience, words, sounds, straight down, into obscurity.

Somewhere farther, much farther than what our eyes can trace after.

They watch the empty spot burnt into that once perfect emptiness.
They have lost their *key* forever.

The moment she pulled herself out of it, everything in the darkness ruptured. Leaving only the waters, still surging.

Water is always the one that survives

(the door opens)

from any transformation, natural or catastrophic, from ice melted, from tears evaporated, from juice expressed, from an apricot sliced ope— From an apricot lies face up in the ceramic plate on a table in a room, for example. The apricot is dried of colors in the resonance of the *absence of a keen eye.*

(a key eye)

She remembers she once was also young and yellow.

13

The missing of the first line opens a grid poem into *roundness.*

A room retrieved from the last mouthful of light fringed by names,
        dimmer,
in the air

of recognition,

pronounced.

Textures swimming in textile

        but your hands still empty with but pastiches.

To punctuate a distance between two mirroring silences with invisibility,
to stand on top of a silence
and become the I

of an exclamation mark—

(exclaimed silence)

slashing apart the flesh of significations

in the room

every word is named by a question,
every word is known by a question,
every word is known but refuses to share the cup of complicity with you.

You lean against this *roundness* of the room. Helpless.

A *round* room excludes all doors, into or out of it.
At once a sea and a dessert, a series
of refractions
from a drop of air, rain-coated.

At once a flood and a draught of textures.

Textures swimming in textile

(You want to take a picture but couldn't fit *roundness* into the viewfinder.)

Textures dancing

Constellation, or *you think they are making fun of you*:

apricot	yellow	applying
paper	sly	separating
stone	ruminating	separating
vase	wide	applying (fast)
fish	rotational	separating
another vase	writing	applying (combust)
square	*round*	applying
quiver	bright yellow	separating
quiver	burnt	separating (slow)
yellow	amniotic	applying
edge	malleable	applying (slow)
apricots	prophetic	applying
reflection	ambivalent	applying (fast)
gravity	entwined	separating (slow)
edges	murmuring	separating
voice	amphibious	applying (combust)
clock	ignorant	separating
breakfast	confessional	separating
end	mortal	separating (fast)
another end	infinite	separating (slow)
apricot	split	applying
fountain	blind	applying
words	molten	applying (slow)
room	oceanic	applying
light	nocturnal	applying (combust)
moon	succulent	applying (combust)
apricot	solar	(slow)
slowness	wet	(combust)
sea	curious	now where?

(You see, nothing is smoother than adjectives)

What you see inside also distorted by the *round* walls.
What you see is an earthrise from the moon you are staring at in the sky.
What you see when you can't help thinking it is yourself sinking.

Roundness is a mantra.

You are in the middle of a *round* poem.

You are not sure what brought you here, but what matters at the moment is to catch the words.

(The stage is so smooth you are slipping away. Slipping into sleep—)

You are desperate for logic.

But there is nothing you can do except for walking *round* and *round* this perfect *roundness*.
Whichever direction you go *roundness* is always behind you.

(If only one word)

if   only one word
if   only one word in front of you is *if*.

(*if* is always reaching out, into)

if you think this chaos is just a joke you made in the first place, or a riddle
if you forget
if it is going to end somewhere
if   what is this space is by nature unanswerable like an answer itself,
a dark window
if you made the joke to her in a dream that you never expected you would
lose control of
if she is convinced
if she stopped she would disappear
if she stopped she would disappear and that
if not a sea, this could only be a theatre but even
if people are all waiting for her to row over, it is not that she has never
imagined that
if all of this is in fact, just a tiny bird, a tiny oracle bird with so long and
confused a tongue where every word grows old before it is rendered into
the air,
if she is one of its thinner veins in its arteries, on its neck, where the blood
appears to be bluer and sweeter, that each time it speaks, the vibration
splits her into two and then into two and then soon she would become a
real tree of language, a time machine, a proud and shattered eye, rain,
like something once occurred and promised to never return

if the bird has accidentally swallowed a book in which each section is
another bird, silenced
if it is just impossible, just impossible to digest, indigestible, my god it's
just impossible, impossible...impossible!
O
if that is the reason the book must never be pronounced else she would
fall apart if this is more than a delirium and you are more than a witness
if she knows where she would see you, staring at her if so
if not,

if   the word is *else*

21

(In the following section, the facing pages should be read horizontally

The stage is covered in mirrors of various sizes. The mirrors should be
tain distance into seeing it as a perfectly executed tessellation yet with
through. A precision is required for this fine point of balance in its

Everything on the stage is a mirror. *The center of the circle also a mirror.*

Above, all the lights are on, pouring downward lavishly but held sus
down by the lightness of the lights.

16 girls on the stage.
They might have distinct looks but the intention that they are playing as
-tical garment and hair set. They are pacing around over the stage.

The choreography of their moves is so complicated that it gives the
tered by nature, like pigeons, (3) walking in a completely random fash
clockwise circular motion as they seem to avoid the center of the
dark hole. As if they are to perform the periphery of something un
lake or. They walk cautiously, solemnly in a subtle but constant
Throughout the entire section, the girls should perform this persis
given. Naturally. Like walking is the equivalent of breathing, at least

as one cross-page,   *as one stage.*)

carefully arranged to the extent that it would trick any eye from a cer-
close examination, the color of the stage beneath could still show
trompe l'oeil.   (The color doesn't matter.)

(The stage could be circular or not, but it is *supposed and thought of* to be.)

pended in the air due to the reflection. The stage appears to be weighed

the same character should clearly be communicated through their iden

impression that they are (1) unaware of the other girls on stage (2) scat
ion. What could be said is that the girls move around in a generally
stage, as if they noticed there an imaginary or metaphorical or actual
fathomable or of *unfathomability* itself through the act of walking. A
scurry. Not unlike certain types of ritual dances performed at a rite.
tent quick short-step movement so long as no specific direction is
in the duration of these pages.

(1) walks into *the center of the stage* and lies down on top *the mirror,* radiating into the space.

(2) walks into the left corner of the stage, or at least she believes she is doing so.
(2) walks into the left corner of the circle, confident that nothing ever exists could remain perfect and circles are no exception. There she sits down (Japanese tea ceremony style) on top of the mirrors, buttock to feet, with her upper body still and strictly upright.

(3) walks into the left corner of the stage, picks up two mirrors and lies down on the flat thighs of the kneeling (2).

(4) walks into the center of the stage, bends her upper body over and peers down *into* the lying (1) and remains in this position until next the direction. She remains so absolutely still in this posture that she starts to feel like a crooked willow or a short lamp post.

(2), unaware of (3), keeps staring into the air in front of her.

(5) walks into the center of the stage, bends her upper body over and peers down *into* the lying (1) and remains in this position until next the direction.

(6) walks into the center of the stage, steps in between (4) and (5), bends her upper body over and peers down *into* the lying (1), then furtively starts pulling the dress of the two girls to herself.

(5) pulls the dress of the two girls around her but only manages to get hold of (6)'s dress.

(7) puts both her hands on the shoulder of (8) as she walks past her. They proceed on walking in this loosely attached position.

(3) raises her hands slowly into the air and stops right below (2)'s cheeks, with the two mirrors in her hand, she starts to play around with them, pointing them to and away from each other, rubbing against, or clashing each other.

(2), unaware of (3), keeps staring into the air in front of her.

(8), not noticing (7), continues walking in her original direction but gets pulled back in (7)'s direction and ends up following her as if falling toward her by the work of gravity. Reluctantly.

(9) and (10) walk into the center of the stage, stop at some distance next to (4), (5) and (6) and starts imitating them: bending
over and peering down *into* the lying (1).

(11) has been walking around the place and kneeling down inter-
mittently, foraging mirrors. Her pace slows down gradually as
she loads herself up with them, which makes her the only one
off-beat from the unified rhythm of their individual marches.

(The sound of their flat shoes against the mirrored surface is always in the background of the performance as a drumming or
drone.)

When finally she can hold no more mirrors, she stops walking,
stops *perpetually* (this takes active effort of course.)

(8) puts both her hands on the shoulder of (13) as she walks past
her. They proceed on walking in this loosely attached position.

(8) still not noticing (7).

(5) keeps attempting to pull a second dress and finally now, gets hold onto that of (9). (9) is dragged closer and closer to the entangled cluster of (4), (5) and (6) and while she moves toward them, she is also caught onto the dresses of the other girls she passes by. (10) joins the circle of observers hovering around (1) as well.

(1) lies still and cold in the center of the circle.
(1) lies still and cold *on* the center of the circle, it is her first night on an operation table but she seems exceptionally used to being deprived of agency. She looks peaceful as a sleeping stone. This is a dreamless night. They are not putting anything into or out of her. Oddly she feels the warmth of a spring garden shower under this blaring cold gaze from the shadowless lamp. Peaceful.

(Is it because of the pale green hues she is beginning to see everywhere around her?)

(5) thinks she is waiting for (1).

(13), not noticing (8), continues walking in her original direction but gets pulled back in (8)'s direction and ends up following her as if falling toward her by the work of gravity. Reluctantly.

(13) puts both her hands on the shoulder of (14) as she walks past her. They proceed on walking in this loosely attached position.

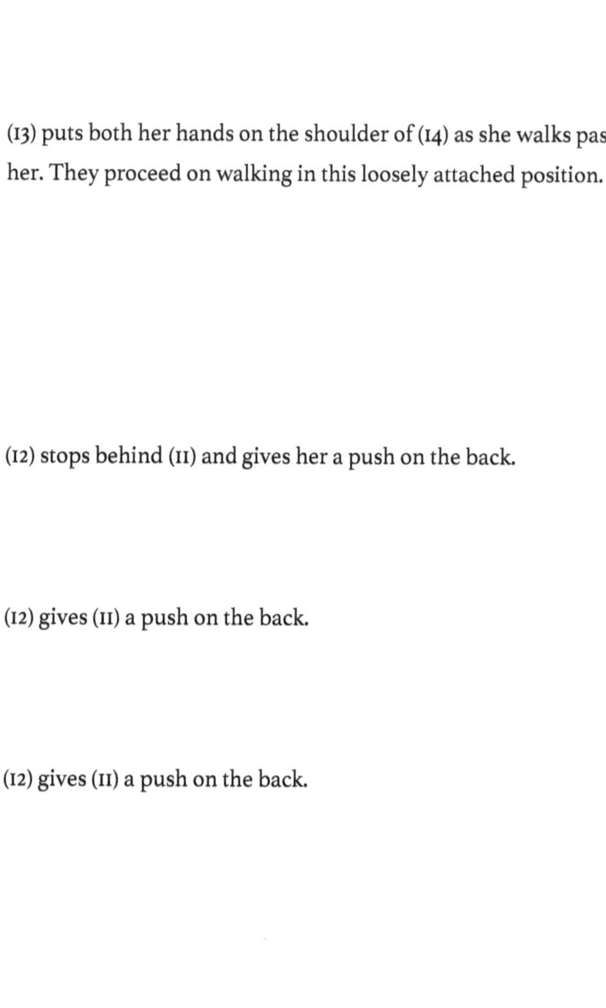

(12) stops behind (11) and gives her a push on the back.

(12) gives (11) a push on the back.

(12) gives (11) a push on the back.

(This pulsating between the two girls continues until (11) has but one last mirror left in her arms. (12) would not stop pushing her, but she holds onto it tight enough that it won't drop. Or maybe because this mirror has become a part of her body already.)

(14), not noticing (13), continues walking in her original direction but gets pulled back in (13)'s direction and ends up following her as if falling toward her by the work of gravity. Reluctantly.

(11) staggers, moves one step forward and drops one mirror from her arms.

(11) staggers, moves one step forward and drops one mirror from her arms.

(11) staggers, moves one step forward and drops one mirror from her arms.

(14) puts one hand on the shoulder of (15) as she walks passes her. They proceed on walking in this loosely attached position.

(3) raises her hands even higher, now in front of (2)'s face. The two mirrors cover up her face completely.

(14) puts the other hand on the shoulder of (4) who is a part of the circle around (1) and managed to keep walking in this position, pulling the entire circle of girls after her, though with apparent unease.

(14), not noticing (15), continues walking in her original direction but gets pulled back in (15)'s direction and ends up following her as if falling toward her by the work of gravity. Reluctantly.

((2)'s countenance is not visible but she is still unaware of (3).)

(The circle formed around (1) gets tighter and denser over time and the pulling force leads them into a centripetal movement. The girls are on the verge of tripping over and stepping onto (1).)

(1) lies in the *meadow* of the night.
Waiting for the dream to recede.

(5) thinks she is waiting for (1) to wake up so she can tell her something, a message maybe, a word, yes a word, but can recall neither the word nor if this premonition is credible at all. So she pulls the dresses to herself more, in a vain hope that one of these girls has stolen and hidden the answer somewhere in them.

(11) still holding the last mirror in her arms: it is *the* mirror who reflects all the light into the place, into the night. The sleep that doubles her dream.

Tonight is a full-mirror night.

She is now at the very front edge of the stage.

(12) stands behind (11), immersing herself in the same sweet illusion with (11) that is exuding from the contour of her held arms.

Suddenly (1) rises from the center of the circle.

(*Did she?*)

(12), shocked by the sight of the silently approaching crows now so close to her she could not see a light, takes a large step backwards but ends up bumping into (11).

As (14) continues to drag (4), the circle begins to move along gradually. The stage is now a fully interconnected whole, transformed into a massive but subtle mechanism. Somber motion flows through the constellation of girls and the hydrography of fabrics the way shells and stick come to life on a navigation chart. The original setting of the stage has collapsed into a fine chaos with mirrors scattered around the place, billowing. Some shattered and some askew: therein, the girls look like crows with horribly oversize beaks.

(The only still point in the scene is the left corner where (2) and (3) rest.)

The trail of girls attached to the circle slides slowly toward (12) from behind. (12), awakened by the looming sound, turns around.

(11) drops off the stage in a sharp shriek.

And all the girls drop, to the stage, accompanying a dramatically loud splash, so loud that you wonder if it was a lump of the moon that has dropped into the sea.

You must also drop, because the lights are out and it is time for intermission.

You must also drop, you are all wet.

Only (1) is still floating *on the surface.*

Notes:

1. All of the actresses are dressed in a long silky yellow sleeveless dress.
them, wiping off their reflected images from them. The reflected
creating a dazzle.

2. Despite the similar appearance of the actresses, the color of their
(3) should be blond and (5) should have velvety black hair (though the
it would think it could well be a silvery grey or even white, or some

3. It was full moon that night when they entered the stage.

The hem of their dresses sweeps around on the mirrors as they go over
lights are also blocked from time to time, the stage dims and relights,

hair differs.
lights bouncing off make it seem less plausible) but anyone observing
thing else than the black.

34

The water is building up,

        the day is wearing down.

Look at your palm, you will see the same forking-converging streams be-ing drawn there, interlacing lines trace over each other, revealing or to retreating into sheer alibi, of themselves or themselves in the future. Time is engraved there. In a pair of facing palms, time is experienced vis-ually, directly. Even the most subtle, gradual shift is captured, consumed, then integrated into this fine mechanism of flowing lines. You never con-sidered this potential reality of everything happening all at once like an explosion at every instance before you read into them.

hand: a palimpsest or fate machine

You think you are reading a book that you would never be able to under-stand.
When you hold one hand next to the other, the words spill immediately toward the other end before you could make out their orders. In this book, the only significance is the instances. Shattered water exists only in instances: you have to read them without reading into them before they lose themselves to the whole once again. Each instance, each mi-nute duration of water you discern there becomes a line, or an illusion of a line, engraved onto this diptych slate, though not by your pronouncing eye but from your recollecting eye: it all begins in recollection, time de-scending backwards. You look at the lines, and feel like hearing the storm of everything and everything impossible falling heavily onto you.

Yes, this must be the great lost mirror whose reflection precedes the world. A reflection that gives birth. Where time is foreseen and enfolded into a two-dimensional plane, filled with the sand of signs. They must be searching for it. What should you do with it? What would they do if they discovered it on you? You are startled. You have no answers. You can but watch the lines continue to propagate into a full chorus of premonition.

Loud and heavy.

You find it harder and harder to distinguish your own hand there among the words.
When you hold them up in front of your eyes they do not appear abnormal, nor do they hurt. Nothing peculiar you notice: You simply do not notice them anymore. They are, absolutely, your *hands*, but what does it mean, a *hand*? It is a strange feeling, like losing your own name to someone else. Or, to a bottomless obscurity. Dropping it, into a night well. Your consciousness dropping into another space, another sky at the end of the well. The lines keep getting louder.

hand: another door.

Your consciousness dissolving. The conceptual contour of your *hand* dissolving—emitting rays of destinies and stillborn destinies into a larger container. A larger hand, so large it is impossible to be confirmed by mortal eyes. Your hands diffuse in a soft reddish whisper, but to their ears this whisper is as urgent and horrifying as a siren. They hear their

Sun dying in the whisper, and in multiples. They are hearing lights reflected on their conceptual skin, smudging it, whitewashing it.

[ALL LIGHTS ARE OFF]

Everyone should evacuate to the periphery of day, immediately.
Repeat. Everyone, should evacuate to, the periphery, of day.

IMMEDIATELY.

They do not find it much different from other peripheries: Covered in a thin coat of the penumbra, an ambivalence in the disguise of dark waters always waiting beyond it, it is not possible to tell where exactly the edge lies. Yet the very moment one steps beyond it, immediately there is nothing but darkness—a dimensionless, directionless, pure perception of darkness.

IMMEDIATELY.

They do not find it much different from other peripheries: Piped with a thin coat of *penumbra*—an ambivalence in the disguise of dark waters, always waiting right beyond—it is not possible to tell where exactly the edge is laid. Yet the very moment one traverses it, there will be nothing. But darkness. A dimensionless, directionless, pure perception of darkness. Immediately you feel it and you know you crossed the line. You feel the darkness not anywhere around but rather, within you. It becomes you. Or maybe, you have become it, taking over its role as the silent observer of finitude, infinitely performed until the next sacrifice step into it.

IMMEDIATELY.

(Perhaps even this darkness is an illusion.)

Among them stands a young female. She has nothing on her that could be called a garment except for a box-shaped cap on her head. Despite so there is no sign of cold or unease on her face. In fact, on the contrary, they find her looking extremely placid, almost as enwrapped in a soft radiance—it is probably her bright blonde hair draping over her though.

But if only anyone dared stepping closer to her, they would realize that it is, instead of her hair, a cascade of pale gold muslin veils running down from the back end of her cap, all the way to her thighs.

The cap, or maybe more precisely, the mask, goes around her face, covering it up entirely, which gives them a huge relief: Her face is an opened coffin through which life and death waft in and out and exchange messages in absolute silence. Nobody has the courage to look into it without the protection of enough grief in their hearts.

So they look at her without seeing her.

Even if the cloth her cap is made of is as diaphanous as dew.

They tell each other that it is the surreal intensity of the pallid light shining through her cap that bereaved them of their sight.

She stands still and expressionless. Unaware of, or indifferent to, their whispers as if standing on another plane of time. A higher plane.

She is the prophet.

A prophet is a king without a kingdom. Or, that without the need to possess a kingdom: Everything here falls to her words, not even desiring to know from which pair of lips these words are from, bewildered but content.

They have no desire to know from which pair of lips these words are from.
They only hear them, even more accentuated in the solid darkness. They hear her presence, in her invisibility, against the darkening sky. Now coalescing into the black waters, dangerous waters, now confused waters, now everywhere.

An echo.

(A true prophet is the corpse of the *fear.*)

They see her everywhere in the expanding dark.
(In reality, what they see is the looming shape of their own fears.)

Some believe they see her lips move, and so comes a low crackling, the burning sky, curling up from its yet—or ever—imperceptible edges. Some see her rising in a constant consumption of light, the crescent waxing fast out of control, bleeding into, eating up their camouflage of night, so deadly seductive...

Some see this *round* ark they huddle on starts silting along with the gushing lights and themselves gliding towards the greater *roundness* beyond. Or that the trees, stretching too long in their shadows, pierce into the shadow of the sky, where the shadow of the stars would fall, raining heavy lapses of temporality, striking on the back of their shadows, striking them into an illusive departure from this catastrophe. Leaving their true bodies below, bedazzled.

They see themselves one after another rising from their deep slumber to a curious dance, swirling like particles released from a metaphysical pause into the true air. Enchanted air. They are not sure if they are dancing to worship something or simply to escape the cold arrows of the shooting stars. They could not make of their own moves. They only know that they have no choice but to keep moving, keep dancing until bumping into someone else—where they will become a new fruit. A new circle is the only exit from this circle.

And she would be hovering at the peak of this delirium. Still invisible in her mesmerizing glow. Still invisible as well, the silvery dance staff held up high in her hand.

...

(this feverish rain will last for quite a while.)

She is sitting alone by the verge of *sea*, throwing pebbles into the sky when you finally find her.

You watch the dainty round stone fly from her like time and skip a brief elegant curve, but soon sinks into the depth of night without a sound. It would have made a perfect skim if it was tossed onto the opposite surface, you regret, quietly to yourself. There her stones are swallowed one after another, surrendering themselves into the infinite sum of possible skies. Will they ever descend again, in the form of tiny droplets or girls? She doesn't seem to be concerned about this, her face still unstirred like the ravenous sky. How many stones has she been feeding it? There is no way you could tell. (Maybe this gesture is no more than a sheer signifier of something else, something more profound, less easily observed with these eyes.) The circle of naked earth gradually revealing itself beneath the pebbles around her indicates that she has been doing this for some considerable time though.

White smooth earth.

She looks like a floating island among the remaining stones and makes the stones appears more plausible as a kind of sea than this *sea* around the day itself.

A floating island on the edge of the edge of the day.

A fleeting island on the edge of the edge of the day, fleeting as a thought.

An afterthought.

Then you realize you have not asked, nor could you have managed to ask, her reason for doing this. You are not even able to convince yourself you have really met that girl.

When you turn around toward the source of your remembrance of her, there it is drained and empty. Leaving only a shallow, dried trench, or the impression of one, at the bottom of your index finger, flat and muted.

Outside (where?) someone is passing by, she could tell.

No. Someone's approaching. Closer and closer he comes, straight at her. She could not hear his steps for sure. It is his shadow that she is hearing—the shadow she casted within him, from him, as she sits there, silverly, releases her body into the vast, monotonous soliloquy of the night. To her ears, everyone is their own shadow.

Now he is only a few steps away from the door, she can tell. There is a voice in the shadow now, speaking but a senseless loose string of words, sprinkling down as his shadow stretches, pulling apart the fine line. Senseless but sharp, burning.

Now he is at the door.

She holds her breath and lets it shower all over her last snow of lights.
And melt.
(It never occurred to you that one could plant their own death)

And harvest it.

When the knob finally turns in his hands, it is freezing.
Almost too cold to be a part of a door.

The door cracks open. But no one is in there. All he finds is a worn-out face, the face of an elderly in the middle of the room. The annihilated face of time at its repose. An apocalyptic piece of *roundness* in a blank space which now resembles an even vaster *roundness*. Too smooth to be measured. There is no way back now, both *front* and *behind* dive into *roundness*, and disappear, like they never once existed.

He couldn't even find the door he has just entered.

He looks at time's closed but weary eyes. No response.

The face he's looking for is nowhere to be found. Not present, at least not seen.

This space is wiped out, the moment he opened it.

IMMEDIATELY.

An echo.

55

She knows what she is waiting for, or what is waiting for her.

CHORUS: the door,

> *behind the door.*

She knows it even better than her own name.

What is a name after all? For one who performs, to take a name as given and eat it, chew it, swallow it down with water is no more than a daily ritual. You don't even think much about the reason anymore once you habituate yourself to the move. You don't ask for the reason anyway, that's the etiquette. You don't stop a sheep halfway on its galloping over the insomniac and ask the story of his name do you? You just follow, and keep the counters going. A sum is enough. You don't even need to get the numbers right. In fact what is important is exactly in the dissolve of the numbers. To respect anonymity is a convention in any space of obscurity. Let the poor thing go. We are, after all, nothing beyond messengers from a plain to another, from costumes to costumes, from names to names, from forgetfulness to forgetfulness. What is the next line?

She wants to say that she has never for once comprehended her name before she was given a new one, so it is as simple as taking off a hat and replacing it with another. The reality is, though, when you wear a name it gets hold onto you, or at least a portion of you, and when you exchange blood (it is like a trade with Satan yes) you become *one*, or at least a portion of you (plural) and there is no way you can get rid of a name you've taken up completely.

you are what you eat.

She thinks of the tears and another girl she swallowed a few days ago and feels a huge disgust.
Maybe it is better to think of names as exterior organs or a kind of integument. One of those tiny golden stone fruits drooping at the end of your hair, one of the many Suns we used to have in the sky? At least it never gets into your bones. She thinks. Isn't that a perfect counterargument? Seldom do you find someone attached to a name when they are cremated. We are all anonymous in fire or ashes. We are all ashes, after all.

stars and stones from the same substance
night and day share the same eye
she and key
forever waiting to be
inserted to that glowing
hole

in its eye she witnesses the wedding of the last
and the first

She walks slowly to the middle of the stage, finds herself a comfortable position, lies down, and wait for the ceremony to begin. Okay. A witness. For the end of the world and the dream of genesis? I can do this. She thinks, closing her eyes. After all she has plenty of time.

> *clouds folding onto its back disposing rain into*
> *the empty*
> *borders of the sky*
> *where things fall from one half to the other*
> *birds hide among the spill*
> *playing the germs of knowledge*
> *in the wind*
> *everything is ignorant*

All but more names. Eventually they will all be stripped down to hollow names when it comes. Fall to the ground. And it will. Yes. Then, there will be a whole carpet of molts, a house of molts, a field of molts...And one moment later, water, no molts, everywhere puddles of water. Then, they will return. Then, nothing. Eventually.

Stage is such a pregnancy projected into space. She thinks. And she is trapped within.

When was she born?

Such a pregnant pause in space withholding a full body of manifestation of life and death and stones and girls and what all within itself.

She contemplates this pregnancy that refuses to offer any response. A pregnant silence, gulping and throwing up itself into but itself. How many lives has she conceived and disposed of in this giant womb? Forget about the numbers. She wonders if the moon has an age and if she feels weaker in her 17711th waxing comparing to her first and her second first. And waning? She feels exhausted even imagining that and having to diary all these useless details. How could anyone imagine not forgetting anything? She decides to imagine something else.

to swim. or a landing dream.

She considers the idea of committing a suicide. But soon decides it was just a whim of nostalgia. Perhaps she was missing one of her sisters. Somewhere far behind. She remembers preferring that name to this one now.

a kaleidoscope of girls

She resumes watching, tired even of wandering off from her duty.

She watches the belly swells even larger.

She thinks hers might have been swelling as well, into something more abstract. Peeling away from

a dance, or a harvest

MEMORIES:
One. Once she performed reading and she thinks in the book that she imagined reading it says that bodies or human bodies are made up 70% with water. So water must mean anticipation.
Two. She remembers pondering over this idea but soon thought of it unconvincing: She is unquestionably 100% anticipation. Where could the other 30% be?
Three. They'd have nowhere to go.

in its own mouth

More space entering. This space is endless, she thinks, and closes her eyes.

This space is constant, only time is specific.
She imagines picking time up from the floor after the puddles dried. But they are so prickly she could not hold them long. No one can possess it. How romantic to share this lonely eternity with something you know you can never possess for sure? There isn't much certainty in this space after

all. Even a negation is so poignant. Yes time is specific, she thinks, and unruly.

Even if anonymous.

This space is narrow, narrow enough to keep her a prisoner yet still running forward, fast, fast enough to eclipse over any of her attempts to escape. Besides, whereto? What good to leave one name of open desperation into another? Once you escape, everywhere you go and everywhere you are is an escape. Is it really any difference from waiting? Where you find no head and tail on the ring as well. The ring...She thinks she might have played as a satellite before but could not find a solid piece of memory that serves as a proof.

MEMORIES:
Four. She feels like having invented *writing* back then so as to *kill the time* she could not help vomiting due to the nausea from circling the stage too fast or it could be the gravitational force but you see this *writing* was not helping much since somewhere in the process she would either run out of words or lose track of their significance or of their parsing or the lines as they confuse their sequences and compartments and melt into one giant pieces of time spit out again and again and she would find herself burning crashing down from the heavens to the sea of time and it is indeed very hard to spread your arms in something of this consistency.

Five. *Writing* can never outwit time, she wrote. Better not to write love letters to time. It gets you nowhere but deeper into a pathetic nihilism. Six. What good to take one more name of the same waters. Why not just wait for now? They told you to wait.

She wonders where and when could she find the lost 30%.
She is horribly bored. Maybe I will try writing again, she thinks, but in dots this time.
Each word as but an instance.

urgent and chronic

She hears the approaching swelling, filling every corner of the presentiment outside, merely one step away.

(It seems as if this one step is taking forever.)

As if this one step arches over the entirety of time, as if he is the step, and the step before this step: always one step further. Like the word yesterday, the drop she once caught a glimpse of, falling infinitely lighter infinitely slower falling infinitely to but never onto her. She doesn't like the sound it makes.

MEMORIES:

Seven. She realized she could not tell if she was dreading this simple fact under the costume of despair. It is so simple she has no response for it.

Eight. After all she has plenty of time.

Nine. She has never once stepped out of this stage, as far as she remembers. She remembers when he held her left hand and wrote *her* into her right palm, they felt more like *purpose* than the only *life* she knew, and then, she opened *her* eyes.

Ten. Soon they gave her a new name. No one is playing her parents anymore. How could she know more about herself?

After all she has plenty of time. She will keep playing waiting until then. And nothing else she could do, after all.

Waiting is spatial.

As if the door never will be opened.

Her eyes feel heavy now, her senses blurry. But she could not tell if it is her falling from sobriety to sleep or the other way around. From sleep back to anticipation.

She could not tell if she is really *waiting*.

If she is really *waiting* for him to hold her hands again, take the name off her, lay his one hand over hers and make a new *waiting* born, into her.

Or if the new name is *waiting*, in confusion.

Or if the new name is confusion.

After all she has plenty of time

time

89

falling silently
a-*round*

silence is the best *round* of applause

About Atmosphere Press

Atmosphere Press is an independent, full-service publisher for excellent books in all genres and for all audiences. Learn more about what we do at atmospherepress.com.

We encourage you to check out some of Atmosphere's latest releases, which are available at Amazon.com and via order from your local bookstore:

Until the Kingdom Comes, poetry by Jeanne Lutz

Warcrimes, poetry by GOODW.Y.N

The Freedom of Lavenders, poetry by August Reynolds

Convalesce, poetry by Enne Zale

Poems for the Bee Charmer (And Other Familiar Ghosts), poetry by Jordan Lentz

Serial Love: When Happily Ever After... Isn't, poetry by Kathy Kay

Flowers That Die, poetry by Gideon Halpin

Through The Soul Into Life, poetry by Shoushan B

Embrace The Passion In A Lover's Dream, poetry by Paul Turay

Reflections in the Time of Trumpius Maximus, poetry by Mark Fishbein

Drifters, poetry by Stuart Silverman

As a Patient Thinks about the Desert, poetry by Rick Anthony Furtak

Winter Solstice, poetry by Diana Howard

Blindfolds, Bruises, and Break-Ups, poetry by Jen Schneider

Songs of Snow and Silence, poetry by Jen Emery

INHABITANT, poetry by Charles Crittenden

Godless Grace, poetry by Michael Terence O'Brien

March of the Mindless, poetry by Thomas Walrod

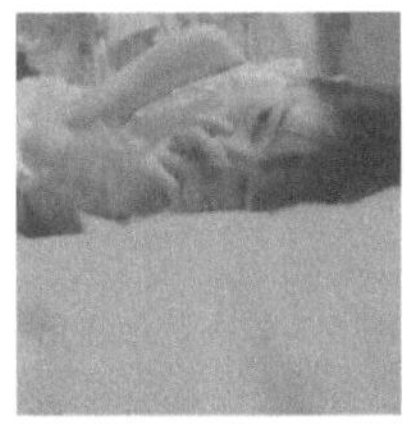

Author's Bio

煦 (Susie Zhu) is a multi-hyphenated poet-artist based in Providence, RI, who's profoundly confused by everything (including her own works, which confuse genres.) She mainly produces "books", in which a "book" refers to its most extensive, abstract, even obscure signification, including but not limited to: text, artist's book, sound, music, video, installation, and performance. Her "books" are encapsulated time-space for meditation and contemplation, where she explores the alternatives for perception and expression.

煦 is the recipient of Accent Accent International Poetry Award for Emerging Voice, Frances Mason Harris '26 Prize for book-length manuscript of poetry and prose, the chief editor of Clerestory Journal of the Arts, and the founder of Butter*Rabbit*Press. Her works have appeared in multiple literary and art journals and have been exhibited around the world.

Some relics of her works could be found at moon-to-suisei.com .